Boxing the Compass

by Sandy Florian

Noemi Press
Las Cruces, NM

This book copyright © 2013 by Sandy Florian.

LIBRARY OF CONGRESS CATALOGING-IN-PUBLICATION
DATA AVAILABLE UPON REQUEST

ISBN 978-1-934819-28-9

Cover design by Ed Ortega
Interior design by Mike Meginnis

Published by Noemi Press, Inc.,
a nonprofit literary arts organization

www.noemipress.org

For My Parents

BOXING THE COMPASS

$0°$

A wind rises, *tramontana, levante, ostro, poniente,* but the points come from the directions of the eight major, eight half, and sixteen quarter notes. The Chinese divide the compass by the signs of the Zodiac, *rat, rabbit, horse, rooster,* but for the more western apprentice, the first thing to know is the name. North is indicated by the spearhead above the *t,* but the *t* soon evolves into the lily-like fleur-de-lys. Then the *l* is replaced with a cross, linking east with the ambivalent direction of paradise, to the place where Christ was born. Colors on the compass are the result of the need for clarity, rather than a mere cartographical whim. So on a rolling ship at night, by the light of the flickering yellow lamp, the figure in the distance becomes visible as she

unfolds her body the same way some people unfold letters from their lovers who've set sail, slowly, with caution, minding the curled edges of the cracked pages, that fading blue ink of time. She unfolds herself from her middle, then opens her yellowed arms and legs, one by one, as if the letter had been folded in halves, quarters, and eighths. She unfolds herself, opens her eyes, and focuses on the blurred pages. Words still. Mind clears. She reads.

Because the color stands out, the eight principle points are shown in black. Half winds are typically depicted in blue or green. Quarter winds are typically depicted in ruby. So on a rolling ship at night, by the light of the flickering lamp, the figure in the distance unfolds her body the same way some people unfold sails, yes, minding the frayed edges of the fraying wind. She opens her canvas arms and legs as if the sail had been blown, *tramontana, levante, ostro, poniente,* but the wind keeps changing directions. Words still, mind clears, but the wind, *greco, sirocco, libeccio, maestro,* words still, mind clears, and she wants to be named by the lying down element, but it's her name that keeps changing, her body. She lies in a bed that measures four leagues by eight leagues, she lies in a bed that measures thirty-two leagues squared. This is the box in which she beds.

Between each point and the next are quarters, but even the careless observer will see that the first is dead ahead, followed by a point on the starboard bow, followed by two points on the starboard bow, followed by three points on the starboard bow, followed by four. Words still, and her soliloquy, her silhouette is framed at the frame, framed in the window, framed in this box, framed in the bed, framed in that well of sleep, that shell, that hole, the spell of the dream she had of assembling the petals of a well-known flower, *one one-thousand, two one-thousand,* losing her rows of teeth. Her rotation defines her orientation, *three one-thousand, four,* as she sits at the edge of her bed

now counting the bones in her mouth, *five one-thousand, six,* along with the cardinal directions that correspond to degrees. And here, there is no accomplishment more ephemeral than this image, here, and as she sits, frayed and framed at the well, at the hole, at the shell, not noticing through the window the new spring tree covered in bottle green buds, counting again the bones in her mouth, *seven one-thousand, eight,* not noticing the white wings of an airborne plane against the bare blue sky, *nine one-thousand, ten one-thousand,* not noticing the uncommon occurrence of a silver dove now fluttering its wings on a branch of the tree, through the framed box window facing north,

11°15′

now weeping. A flat puppet of magnetic steel, she pigeons on her pivot, turning her inward thoughts toward the door, now open, now closed, and she does so in consequence of being so reluctantly aware of herself. Though she speaks to no one, she wishes to present her own hypocrisy. Though she speaks to no one, she invites them to read the Bible, Plato, Montaigne. She speaks to no one yet argues that Plato himself articulates the arbitrary rules by which she naturally studies the laws of the city in which she now lives unnaturally, uncivilly, and because her translation of the world is similar to Plato's, she thinks her deficits are also similar, and so she dismisses herself. For she too is guilty of leaning too heavily on the tomb of truth. But this only is a minor viewpoint. The more important point of view is the view from the moon where

the loom of the oceans is more readily apparent, these oceans upon which her bed now shifts and drifts, that drifting continental drift, across these oceans wide that cover more than two thirds of the surface of the Earth and host its hurricanes, cyclones, and tsunamis. But this is only a minor viewpoint. The more important point of view is the minute-by-minute version, conversion, of the image illumined by flicker on the box-springed bed where the body is now

gone because in the corner of the room she picks up her clothes
from the clutter in the room and moves herself through this ocean,
branch by slow branch, limb by slow limb, wishing for a moment she
had time for a bath, then dismissing this wish with the somnolent   sleepy.
memory of a wayward song from a wayward piano. From the clutter
in the corner, she picks up the shirt that once belonged to her father,
her lover, her brother, though she can't remember ever having a
brother, a lover, a father—the shirt she now wears, now tattered and
torn. But the more important point is the question of whether the
truth of the moment can be presented, represented by clock and
by compass. When he wore it the canvas was white. The canvas
was intact. Now the canvas is yellowed and frayed at the neck, as
she gathers this tattered shirt in the waist of her worn jeans, the
jeans from the clutter, now bluing, now fading, as she gathers herself
inside the folds of the room, the closed door, now open, and spills
herself onto

that ocean predominating this world of ice and fog and lake and
stream, crashing and clashing with the clouds, circulating between its
phases, by evaporation, by precipitation, by the articulate movements
of the atmosphere, and the downhill flow of rivers, glaciers, and
groundwater that keep spilling through

this simple apartment building in this simple city in which ambiguous
hallways connect dots to other dots and dogs bark their barks behind
the backdrops of yet other doors, now opening, now closing.

When she was a child, she wore a dress that she called her favorite, of
blue hyacinth print against a gleaming white sky, with elastic on the

top and a wide-rimmed skirt. And when the four winds would blow, *tramontana*, *levante*, *ostro*, *poniente*, her dress would billow, inflate, and set sail under the gleaming skies, over the fathomless seas, and blue. This dress was woven by the wind itself, and when it disappeared, she waited under water for days. She waited under water for weeks. She waited under water for years, until she asked her mother, for centuries, who responded in rags. But her ballooning dress never returned and her feet remained bound to the ground, the deep blue vein palpitating from her skull. Her mother. Her mother madly,

who, when she was a child, floated like a buoy at the foot of her well-shaped bed and identified the Pacific, the Atlantic, and the Indian by their arbitrary margins. Margins, she argued, delineated more by human history and geographical politics than by currents and biological populations. She listened with a silent caution, listening to the waves cresting and falling, flowing and wending, as she pointed with her finger to the looming map of the world, where in the southern hemisphere, one of these arbitrary margins extends southward to Antarctica from the hopeful Good Hope, where another stretches southward from the horned Cape Horn, where the third passes through Malaysia and Indonesia to Australia and on to Antarctica, pointing with her finger and proving resolutely that only arbitrary margins separate her from

the ambiguous hallway and the dogs that bark and bark behind the backdrops of doors still opening, still closing, as if area-volume analyses could be made, should be made, between these individual regions of life.

And who told her how, in the early 20th century, a man named Kossina had an unrelenting desire to map the bottom of the world, and so he collected data from the cannonball soundings taken from cannonball boats, the cannonball data from the cannonball sea, that cannonball data collected by those early explorers, from explorers like Sir John and Sir James who sailed the Arctic and the Antarctic, from explorers like Sir John and Sir James who set their sights upon the sea to map the ocean, to discover the poles, to know the Eskimos and their abodes of snow. Night after night, he puzzled over their maps, folding them, unfolding them, layering them, collaging them, perturbing them, applying them, studying them, hemming them, with his gentle obsession, with his quiet compulsion, night after night by the light of the flickering lamp, folding, unfolding.

She unfolds her body the same way some people unfold sails, yes, by the flickering light of that fading blue ink of time. She unfolds herself, opens her eyes, and focuses on

that simple path in that simple hallway that connects two simple doors, still opening and closing, two distinct doors delineated only by arbitrary margins, listening to the dogs that bark as she spills herself through the landing between these flights of stairs, the overlap of planks, the clinker-built shell, as she spills herself through the distance, between the middle of the rivet hole and the edge of the shape, through the indistinct door, down the concrete steps, and onto the

22°30'

sidewalk, where she turns north-northeast on that landmass, that terra firma that covers merely a third of the surface of the Earth and has a mean elevation of a mere three thousand feet, compared to the ocean's mean depth of thirteen thousand, that landmass so marked by the peak of Mount Everest at a mere twenty-nine thousand compared to the deep nadir of Marina Trench at thirty-six. She turns north-northeast and follows her footsteps over the

sidewalk, concrete composite of limestone and clay embedded with fossilized names encrypted by fingers, fossilized faces and veins of old leaves, now dead, now gone. She turns north-northeast and follows herself over these fossils until she reaches the intersection of two equivocal streets in this equivocal city and waits on the corner for the light to turn green. Dust settles on her as it settled on her broken piano. She was a child when it broke. Now it is her.

And though there is little information on the early history of the Earth's waters, fossils dating from the Precambrian age 3.3 billion years ago prove that bacteria and cynobacteria existed, indicating the presence of water even then. Fossils of primitive marine algae and invertebrates date 540 million years ago. But she doesn't notice the fossils of leaves on the concrete. She doesn't notice that the streetlight turns green, now yellow, now red. Listening to the wayward song on the wayward piano and standing on the corner of this street and that street, she doesn't notice anything at all until the light turns green a second time, and she follows her shadow across the street, up the curb, and onto the opposite

sidewalk, concrete composite of limestone and clay, buckled by relief grooves excavated at intervals in yards, excavated with the intention of minimizing the damage from tectonic shifts and temperature fluctuations. When she was a child, she was careful to walk on the grids of relief grooves, between the yard-long squares of concrete. She carefully stepped on the grids of grooves because stepping on the tiles themselves would have sent her plummeting to a lake of pebbled crocodiles snapping their pebbled jaws, those crocodiles that congregate in the shallows of ponds and lakes, those crocodiles that feed on the flying birds, their close relatives, with their identical four-chambered hearts. Those pebbled crocodiles whose lineage dates 200 million years, along with the dinosaurs, but unlike dinosaurs these cold-blooded crocodiles survived Earth's greatest extinctions, only to find themselves lurking between relief grooves of every ambiguous city.

When she was a child, she walked carefully on the grids of grooves, step-together-step, because on a rolling ship at night, by the light of the directional lantern, the red beads of those crocodile eyes flicker, blink, and gleam against the still black lake, carefully avoiding the flickering eyes at the bottom of the flickering lake, those flickering crocs that swallow rocks and hard stones in order to better chew their prey. She walked ever so gently until she received, without warning, a frenetic sharp tug. Come here. Come now. And she wants to remain here and forever and always walking ever so gently north-northeast, but it's her name that keeps changing, her body, this body of ocean and ocean floor.

And though there is little information on the early history of the Earth's waters, she does know that lakes form as a result of those same tectonic shifts and temperature fluctuations. That they're temporary bodies of water that open and close, swell and recede, appear and disappear in a breath. And on the 3rd of June in 2005, a lake in Russia sunk into the earth in a matter of minutes. Officials theorized that this disappearance was caused by a shift in the soil that pulled like a plug and drained like a snake, through narrow channels that lead to rivers that flow through every ambiguous city. Because lakes are temporary bodies of water that open and close, and when they close, they form fens of peat, spongy vegetation, and moss, until the green trees grow and turn wetlands into forests.

Similar to a bog.

33°45'

And if there are any signs on the door of the bakery that read "Hours of Operation: 7 am to 7 pm," or "This is the Time of Your Life," she doesn't notice, because the only thing she notices is the heaviness of the door, of the clock, of the compass, the heaviness of her eyelids as she walks to the counter, and

Morning miss. What'll it be today?

A half a loaf of raisin bread please. This is my empty body.

A half a raisin? Anything else?

No, no, just the half. This is my empty box. For though she speaks to no one, she encourages them to remember that it was Socrates who declared he hungered not for matters of the body but for matters of the soul, that it was Socrates who argued it's the fault of the body that we are so broken, so sick and forsaken, that it was Socrates who said it's the body that distracts and impedes and thwarts with its endless requirement for bread.

No, no, just the half, just the miracle of five small loaves and two small fish, because although she looks at no one, she encourages them to remember that it was Jesus who blessed and broke the bread, it was Jesus who blessed and broke the fish, it was Jesus who distributed it to a multitude of people, so blessed and so broken, ambling the barren desert, halfway across the barren Earth.

No, just the half, just the matter of eggs and flour and yeast and water, just the miracle of milk and raisins and sea salt and sugar, and though she hears no one, she remembers her mother, her mother madly, as she stirred, mixed, and kneaded the dough, as she shaped, baked, and rose the bread. She remembers her mother drifting on the continental drift, floating like a buoy, like a bright orange buoy, at the edge of the stove that measured thirty-two leagues squared, floating like a buoy at the edge of the stove and telling her

that although there is little information on the early history of that superocean, Panthalassa, we do know that 200 million years ago, the supercontinent, Pangaea, broke into parts that drifted across the Earth and opened the mouths of the Atlantic and the Indian Oceans, that 140 millions ago, Africa broke from South America, and that at the same time, India and Madagascar broke from Australia and Antarctica. She remembers her mother baking the bread at the edge of her baking bed and saying that it was only 80 million years ago that North America broke from Europe, that Australia broke from Antarctica, and that India broke from Madagascar to drift northward toward Asia, forming the Himalayan Mountain Range, yes,

the Himalayan Mountain Range, the Earth's highest of haunts, that abode of snow that hosts over 100 peaks. The continental journey is not yet complete and that India continues to travel northeast by north at a rate of 2½ inches per year, at the rate of the growth of your fingernail, she said, floating like a buoy, do you see how your fingernail so slowly grows? And that over the next 10 million years, India will travel another 1000 miles to land right in the middle of Asia. She remembered finding herself terrified by the drift, so slowly floating at the edge of a full-blown stove, drifting away at the rate of the growth of a nail, with the slow resolution of rising bread. That'll be three dollars and fifty-two cents, no,

no, just the half, and how in the early 1960s, a man named Harry Hess with a countenance discovered that new oceanic crust is still forming as a result of the ovens of active volcanoes that erupt at the crests of ocean ridges, those many marine mountains that flow snake-like across 40,000 miles of the very bottom of the ocean. That molten matter erupts from these ovens where it then cools, hardens, and solidifies and is pushed aside by the newest intrusions. And that later that same decade, this discovery of seafloor spreading was merged by geologists with the discovery of the drifting continents, formulating the basis of Plate Tectonic Theory.

Miss? Excuse me?

Yessorry?

That'll be three dollars and fifty-two cents.

Oh, yes. I'm sorry. I was just . . . I was just . . . trailing off here, I was just drifting on this divisive shift. I was just trying to remember. No, I was just trying to

Out of five?

forget, and if there are any signs on the door of the bakery that read "Many Marine Mountains are Always Erupting," or "This is the End of Time," she doesn't notice, because the only thing she notices is the heaviness of the newspapers stacked at the edge of door, the heaviness of the day, the hour, the minute, as she pushes the heavy door and steps onto the

45°

sidewalk turning northeast on that landmass, concrete composite of
well and of shell, of hole and of bowl, of buds from that ever budding
past, so buckled by history and crumpled by memory, so embedded
with the remnants of crocodile eyes crying crocodile tears on these
crocodile days when she steps onto the sidewalk and turns northeast
on that landmass, embedded with bone and embedded with stone and
embedded with the sharpest of shark-like teeth, gritting and gripping
and pivoting on land, like a lazy puppet of magnetic steel, like a pigeon,
a pirate, a steel colored dove, stepping and crawling and erasing the
page as words still, mind clears, and she reads onward and forever
because she wants to stay here and forever and always, but this is the
box in which she spirals, yes, this is the box in which she turns northeast
onto that mass, onto that past, this is the box in which she crawls and
gnaws across the page at the rate of the growth of a fingernail, at the
rate of the growth of a strand of hair, she step-together-steps and turn-
around-turns on the biggest of boats over fathomless seas whichever
way the wind might whisper away, *greco, syroco, africus, maestro,* whirling
and curling and cording her way, creeping and crawling at the rate of a
strand, twirling and gliding like a full-blown stove, growing and inching
and rising in spirals, looming and blooming and cresting and falling,
puzzling with wonder which way the wind, crying crocodile tears on
this crocodile street of this crocodile city where ambivalent doors

connect lines to straight lines, in rectangles and squares, while, running in circles, dogs bark as they bark, they yelp and they yowl, and they bay as they prey to the ambivalent moon through some ambivalent window in this ambivalent world blowing which way the wind, as she pushes the heavy door and blows onto the

sidewalk, turning northeast on that line that connects two arbitrary doors of those arbitrary margins, listening to the barks of good dogs and the chirps of sweet birds, when, come here, come now, a woman through the gap of a window whistles, a woman through the gap of a window sings, a woman through the gap of a window now raises her arm, white and snow-milk against a sill of slow brick, a woman through the gap of a window now slams the window shut. She was a child when it broke. Now it is

56°15′

high noon.

The principles of the Plate Tectonic Theory are that the interior of the Earth is made up of two major layers, the lithosphere of crust and of mantle and the asthenosphere of molten magma. The lithosphere is then composed of eight major plates that ride on top of the asthenosphere and move in relationship to one another at one of the convergent, divergent, or transform boundaries where they quake and erupt and form mountains and trenches.

The convergent boundary, her mother taught her, is like two people walking precisely toward each other and finally colliding. The divergent boundary, her mother explained, is like two people walking away from each other and finally separating. The transform boundary, her mother continued, is like two ships that pass in the night, *so quietly 'neath the stars' soft light*, as she moved ever so gently into her own gentle dream.

It's like two people, her mother once said. It's like two people passing each other on the sidewalk. It's like this. It's like you and this woman walking toward you right now. Look at this woman walking toward you with her hooked back and her unsteady cane. Watch how she grows so steadily in your vision. It's like you and this woman, growing steadily in your vision, growing larger and larger with each passing step. Look how she totters and tips with her hook and her cane. Look how she waddles and twists on her unsteady legs. Look at her bags, and watch how she sags. Watch how she bobbles so blindly toward you.

It's like you and this woman walking toward you, stumbling around like a tumbling rock, fiddling with her memory and trying to remember the dress that she wore when she was a child, of blue hyacinth print on a gleaming white dye, with elastic on the top with a wide-rimmed skirt. Fiddling with her memory and trying to recall the dress that would billow, inflate, and set sail, yes, *tramontana, levante, ostro, poniente*. Look at this woman walking toward you, shifting and drifting and shivering and shaking, stumbling and lumbering and trembling and quaking, lifting to face you and then suspending beside you, Good morning to you. Good afternoon, dangling in time for the briefest of instants before trembling and quaking and rumbling away.

Other people say, her mother explained at her desk with the starfish paperweight, that the only way to explain the movement of the continents is to understand that the world is slowly expanding. Some people believe, she said as she dipped her hands into the top left drawer, the Earth started out small, as she found a flat rubber balloon, like this small balloon, see? before she blew some breath into the blue balloon. Then the Earth was only half its current size, and the whole globe, she said before blowing more breath, breath between breath, formed one continuous oceanless crust, she turned it sideways and upside down. Then she ran her fingers over the balloon, over the entire tiny globe, saying over and over, Like this, you see? It was just like this. Then, little by little, she said pausing to breathe into the blue balloon, the Earth got bigger and bigger, she filled the world with breath, until the continuous continent broke into pieces that drifted apart and filled the world with sea. She carried the balloon higher and higher and higher and higher until all at once

it disappeared.

And when she was a child, this theory of the expanding globe gave her terrors and nightmares as she dreamt of a world so slowly growing, forever ballooning, getting bigger and bigger and rounder and fatter, until, in her mind, the inevitable balloon burst, the inexorable seas dispersed, and the white laced woman through the gap of the window, this white laced woman now raising her arm, the white laced woman luminescent like milk in this world of such sickness, this white laced woman through the gap of a window slams the window shut.

Until she remembers as suddenly as the most sudden explosion, as suddenly as the most sudden burst, the dream she dreamt last night, that nightmare of losing her rows of teeth, of losing her canines, her molars, incisors. She remembers with the suddenness of the most sudden gun, shot by an ever-expanding balloon, shot by the woman in the whistling window, *tramontata, levante,* she remembers with the suddenness of a world gone bad, as she begins to count the bones in her mouth, *eleven one-thousand, twelve,* as she begins to count the moments that pass, *thirteen one-thousand,* as she begins to count the petals of well-known flowers, *fourteen one-thousand, fifteen,* as she begins to count the moons on her fingernails, *fifteen one-thousand, sixteen one-thousand,* those crescent moons that wax as they wane, and they wane as they wax, she counts and counts the bones in her mouth, twisting her tongue right side up, upside down, twisting her tongue around and around, northeast by east on this globe, on this ever-expanding Earth, on this ever engorging globe, turning northeast by east across the street, up the curb and onto the sidewalk, forever and always

67°30'

turning.

And if there are any signs on the road that read "These are the Ever-Changing Theories of Science" or "Board This Ship Without a Rudder," she doesn't notice, because the only thing she notices as she walks east-northeast to her apartment building is the shape of a dove dead at the entrance, like the shape of a brother, like the shape of a father, like the shape of a mother, a lover, a daughter. Like the shape of a dinosaur dead at the entrance, with its deadly identical four-chambered heart, at the foot of the door, now opening, now closing, now opening, now closing, at the foot of the door of her ambivalent building of brick and of block and of line and of square. And she wants to have been a bricklayer once, a layer of row after perfect row, tapping her feet to the metronome, feeling the beat of her perfect pulse, but the only thing she sees as she turns east-northeast carrying a paper bag of paper bread, east-northeast on that land, on this globe, on this orb, on this sphere, the only thing she sees as she turns east-northeast is the shape of a dove dead on the sidewalk, like the shape of a ship propped on a mountain, like the shape of a whale beached on the sand, like the shape of a fish plum out of water. Yes, she wants to have been a bricklayer once, building the walls of symmetrical bricks and stepping ever so gently on grids of relief grooves embedded in the sidewalk of each beating and rhythmic and pulsating city, as dogs bark as they bark and they bay as they pray through the invisible window, to the invisible dove, now flying, now soaring,

now stalling and falling, now pivoting on this rivet of time, because it's the dove that keeps falling from the sky, at thirty-two feet per second per second.

Because she can easily understand wings and tails and feathers and vents in terms of their survival in the sky, in terms of the avian ability to fly. But what can she make of these wings and things as they lay mountainous on the sidewalk floor?

One of god's little creatures.

And though she speaks to no one, she remembers that it was God who said to Noah, Build yourself an ark of cypress and cover it with pitch, for when seven days pass I will send rain down to Earth. And so Noah built the ark, and then they entered two by two. And when those seven days passed, the fountains of the oceans opened, and then the waters rose. And all the windows of all heaven opened, and then the waters rose. And torrents of rain fell from the sky, and then the waters rose. The water rose and continued to rise and rise until it covered all the land and all its mountains, obliterating every living thing on Earth, all of man and all the animals, blotting all the airborne birds of the sky, yes, all those birds that billow, inflate, and set sail, as the woman in the window whistles.

One of god's little creatures, she says, speaking aloud to none but herself, remembering that it was Ea who said to Utnapishtim, Build yourself a boat of wood and cover it with pitch, for when seven days pass I will send rain down to Earth. And so Ea built the boat, and then they entered two by two. And then the fountains opened, the windows opened, torrents of rain fell from the sky, and then the waters rose, and continued to rise until it covered all the land and all its mountains, as a high bird on a high wire holds its soprano.

Excuse me? In god's name . . . what did you say

as the local postman comes out of the blue, the local postman with his local parcel, the local postman with his local place, the local postman with his big blue bin, his big blue bin, so full of words. Words still, mind clears, and she imagines he has a letter for her, a letter from her beggar brother. Dear Catastrophe. It's been a long time. Too long, I've missed you. I am writing you from the bottom of the sea. From this blue bin, so full of words.

And it was Uta who said to Ziusudra, Build yourself a boat, then all the oceans opened, I'm sorry. I didn't mean to say, and continued to rise, in good God's name, it's one of god's little creatures, each living thing, as a passing truck blows its horn.

For when those seven days passed, the oceans opened, the windows opened, and torrents of rain fell from the sky, and then the waters rose and continued to rise as they are rising right now, yes, as they are rising right now.

You know, one of god's little creatures,

78°45′

whose gravity overcomes him.

For though she speaks to no one, she invites them to read the Bible, and Plato, Montaigne, for when she was a child, she attended Bible school on Sunday mornings, Not for the God, her mother would say, but for those glorious stories. And though she has forgotten many of these stories, she still remembers those biblical dreams, those dreams of ladders and ascents to heaven, those dreams of brothers and sheaves of wheat, dreams of cows and ears of grain, dreams of bakers and golden cups. She remembers these dreams as if she had dreamt them herself, as if she had once had a brother, a dozen brothers, as vividly as she recalls the Sunday skirt her mother would sometimes wear,

a flowing skirt of a glowing peach long enough to reach her ankles, and as they walked to Sunday school, she imagined she was really floating through space like an orbiting asteroid or wading through water like a magical mermaid, a neon beacon of magical light, and she named her mermaid Madeline, Madly, for short. She would say to her mother, I love you mother Madly, I love you madly, mother, Madly, you who never bother to dream some sleepy dream, because your life is dreamy enough.

Not for the God, she would say, but for the glory of the story, and although she remembers mostly the dreams, she also remembers Noah, because it was Noah who set free a dove to see if the waters had subsided, but the dove found no place to land and so it returned to the ark. And after seven days passed, Noah set free another dove to see if the waters had subsided, but this dove returned to the ark with just a branch in its beak. And after seven days passed again, Noah set free another dove to see if the waters had subsided. But this dove did not return, for here it lies, dead on the sidewalk,

dead on the sidewalk

90°

of ocean floor.

And if there is any mail collected in the broken bin of this big boat, and if there's a pile of newspapers stacked on the port side of its deck, and if there's any notice on the cork on the starboard side that reads, "Lost: Blue Healer, Blotchy Grey Spots" or "Wanted: One-Way Ticket to Atlantis" she doesn't notice, because the only thing she sees as she wades east through the entrance and east through the hallway is the face of the dove dead on the sidewalk, like the face of a mother all out of true, like the shape of a brother buried in a box, and she wants to have marked the scene of the crime, that patch of catastrophe, with a marker, some tape, police tape, a brick. Because it's the shape of things that stay her, yes, it's the shape of things

that make her stay. And here there is no snapshot more lucid, more crystal clear, than this picture of her and as she stands framed in the hallway of her ambivalent building, framed in the doorway of her numbered apartment, framed in those moments fleeting from word to word and page to page, turning her door-key counterclockwise to the left, reversing that quick clock of time, and though she can think of nothing besides that small death at the entrance, as she turns her door-key counterclockwise to the left, she knows too that her days are numbered, *seventeen one-thousand, eighteen one-thousand* and that these hours and minutes and seconds are mere fleeting memories, *nineteen one-thousand, twenty,* as they wind themselves around this merry-go-round going round and round. She'd like the time to take a bath. But this is just the briefest wish. The more enduring image is this image halfway around the world where a half a dozen fishing boats are moored to a half a dozen piers while half a dozen fishermen lie buzzing in their bunks, for

inside her living room, the phone isn't ringing, the answering machine isn't blinking, the candle isn't burning, and the incense isn't smoking, but the hands of the clock on her mantle keep spinning in succeeding hours and minutes and seconds, one after the other after the other, as if inside her living room there was only this dying, as if inside this living room there was only this pivoting on this rivet of time where birds keep falling from the sky, yes, she turns her door-key counterclockwise to the left, and

stumbles into her living room where framed photographs line up like soldiers on the shelf, pictures of mountains and pictures of valleys, pictures of ruins and seascapes and snow, those lonely abodes, pictures of homes she had lived in, cities she visited, landscapes and landmarks and monuments of weight, she turns her door-key counter to the clock where old photos of old moments line up like old solders reminding her to remember, to reminisce, and to recall,

her father, dear father, that poor heart attack of a man, for here on this shelf, framed in this frame, framed on the mantle, framed in the room, stands a picture of her blurred father standing fixed inside a moment, standing shouldered near a blurred stranger in a blurry raincoat on a rainy day. Yes, framed in this frame stands a picture of her father standing to the right of a man in some blurry city, some raincoat of a man she never once knew. And she asked her father once, Who is this man in the Macintosh? but her father never responded because her father didn't know.

And here stands a picture of her grandmother Luna, her Mama Lunita, as she used to call her, who if she remembers correctly, if she recalls at all, once gave her a watch for her birthday, a small murmuring and digital trick with a rubber-like band and a chronometer mode that she never quite knew how to use. So she asked her Mama Lunita, she asked her Mama Moon, What kind of watch is this here? but her Mama Lunita never responded, because her Mama Lunita never quite knew that it was a diver's, a swimmer's, a fisherman's watch, a watch for submergence under water.

And here stands a picture of herself wearing her diver's, her swimmer's, her fisherman's watch and standing in front of her mother standing in front of a fountain on which a statue is precariously perched, and on this fountain another little bird is also precariously perched. Here, the sun shines brightly casting shadows across the white-bright floor, and she wants to remain here and forever and always turning her door-key counterclockwise, but it's the clock that keeps spinning its wheels, its hands that keep spitting out hours and minutes and seconds, in halves and quarters and eighths, singing its own song in sixteenths and thirty-two seconds. And she asked her mother once, How many minutes can people live underwater? How many hours and minutes and seconds? but her mother responded, No, she said, Nothing, she said, Never, she said, Nobody can live underwater, she said, Not even for a moment, she said, Not anyone, nowhere.

But will there be time for a bath?

For when she was a child she wanted to bury the poor dead bird, the poor dying bird that was lodged between the wall and the washing machine, that poor excuse for a bird that was lodged for days, she remembers hearing it cry for months, she remembers hearing it cry for years, until she looked for a box, a coffin, a casket, like the one in which she buried her brother, her dozen brothers, her single brother, that ghost of a brother she never quite had. Because she wanted to bury to the poor dead bird, so she looked in circles and circles around the house until she found an empty carton of kitchen matches, all incendiary and full of flame. All incendiary, her mother scolded her,

No, not ever, no never. Come here. Come now. You see, boxes are only pleased with boxes. Only boxes are pleased with boxes. Not birds, Silly Milly. Boxes are only pleased with boxes, boxing. If she could only live inside this box. If she could only live inside this frame.

101°15'

Why is the sky? Why the sea? Why are your eyes so cerulean blue? she recalls in this minute-by-minute version, conversion, turning east by south, toward the kitchen, toward the kettle, toward the full blown stove, the same way she remembers her mother turning east by south, toward the kitchen, toward the kettle, toward the full blown stove, here and forever and always, lifting the kettle from the stove, then centering it in the sink, turning its tap clockwise to the right repeating, Why is the sky? Why is the sea? Why am I so cerulean bloo-hoo-hoo?

then lifting the kettle from the sink, turning toward the stove, and sinking beneath her own slow surface, wave after wave after wave, then

centering the kettle on the stove, turning its knob to the wisdom of clocks, hearing the tick-tick-tick of the flint, sinking beneath her own sensibilities, reminding herself to remember, reminding herself to forget, the responses to her mother would eventually present, standing by the stove in her apron checkered red and white.

Because blue light waves are shorter than red light waves, you see, because blue light waves are shorter than red and orange and yellow waves, you see, than all other waves in the rainbow, see, so blue light is more scattered by the molecules in the sky, those teeny tiny molecules of nitrogen and oxygen, and by the molecules in the sea, those teeny tiny molecules of hydrogen and oxygen, by the teeny tiny particles in his big blue eyes, as she began drifting away, rifting adrift, hearing the tick-tick-tick of the flint, centering the kettle on the full-blown stove, that black iron kettle on that round stove ring, and spinning the knob to the clock of high heat, spinning and falling and sinking beneath her own slow surface to watch it sputter, ignite, and catch flame.

A single water molecule consists of two hydrogens and one oxygen fixed by negatively charged electrons that float free. Water molecules stick to other water molecules by bonding, energy that changes when that it gets hot or cold. So as the water begins to warm, she unfolds a tea bag from the tea box, places it in the mug that she carefully calls teacup, and recalls her mother's lesson that fresh water boils at two-hundred-twelve degrees, *twenty-one one-thousand,* that fresh water freezes at thirty-two degrees Fahrenheit, *twenty-two, yes,* thirty-two degrees, for this is the box in which she beds, measuring thirty-two leagues and degrees.

For although she has no memory of reminding herself to buy milk or to buy butter, as the water in the kettle warms, she also recalls the lesson her mother gave her about the freezing of oceans and lakes and of ponds. That when oceans and lakes and ponds freeze over, she said opening the cupboard to retrieve a clear glass, warmer waters still flow beneath the surface of the ice, and filling the glass with water from the tap. This is because water is denser than ice, placing the glass on the kitchen table. Or because ice is less dense than water, opening the refrigerator's freezer door. Water is weird in this way, taking a cube from the tray of ice. Because the bonds in liquid pack water in clumps, dropping the cube in the clear glass of water. The bonds in ice, on the other hand, pack the molecules more loosely, floating the ice to show by example, in hexagonal crystalline lattices,

in hexagonal crystalline lattices, she echoes, briefly recalling that in the winter they made silver hexagonal snowflakes from aluminum paper and hung them from the Christmas trees all out of true.

So when an ocean freezes over, she explained, floating like an icecap in middle of the sea, when a lake freezes over, she said, floating like a fountain in the middle of her mind, when a pond freezes over, like it did that fateful winter. When a pond freezes over, like it did that fateful winter, life is sustained under ice. Yes, life is sustained under ice.

Like the Beluga Whale in the middle of the Arctic Ocean. Like the Arctic Char in the middle of Lake Hazen. Like all the little fish in all the little ponds all over this great land on this ever-expanding globe, for as the water in the kettle warms, this is the box in which she spirals.

Because when a pond freezes over, like it did that fatal winter, when she and her younger brother, the younger brother she doesn't remember having had, that younger brother she can never quite recall, because when a pond freezes over, like it did that fatal winter, when she and her younger brother skated in free-form figure eights on that frozen pond, that midnight pond, that lost and stolen lullaby pond, for this is the brother she can't recall, as the water in the kettle warms, like it did that fateful winter when she and her younger brother, her younger little brother dressed in his navy pea coat and his red wooly hat, her younger little brother with his red-orange hair and his sailor blue eyes, when she and her younger brother skated in freeform figure eights, for hours and days and weeks, like freeform infinities, for weeks and months and years, until the midnight pond fractured, that lullaby surface ruptured, and the water in the kettle, as the kettle centered on the round stove ring, as the water in the kettle centered on the round stove ring rises to a high pitched whistle.

112°30'

Because another property of water that's attributed to bonding is its high capacity for heat. So when heat is applied to water, most of the heat goes to break the bonds that link the molecules together, the result of which is vapor and fog and mist, the result of which is steam and cloud and haze. But only a fraction of the energy actually increases its temperature, her mother continued, allowing the ocean to absorb and release large amounts of heat with little alteration in temperature. It also means that movements of water, those ocean currents, transfer large amounts of heat around the ever-expanding globe.

For when spring came to thaw the ice, that beautiful ice packed in those beautiful hexagonal crystal lattices, when spring came to thaw the ice and melt the water down, was it March, or was it April? She went to look for her brother in that long lost pond, that lullaby pond, in sunny spring when the water was still, when the pond was tranquil, she remembers sitting at the edge of that silver-rimmed pond on windless days in the middle of spring when the pond was still, when the water was smooth, like a plate of glass, like a windowpane, like a crystal mirror all flat and tranquil, sitting at the edge of that far away pond like she was sitting at the edge of a far away world, calling out to the far away sky, Come here, little fishy. Come now, my little friend, calling to her brother in his navy pea coat and his red wooly hat, with his sailor blue eyes and his red, red hair, like she was calling out to the end of time. Because ponds are temporary bodies of water that open and close and open and close.

Come here, my little fishy. Come now, my little friend, and Why am I so cerulean blue? And when they close, they form fens of peat and sponge and moss.

Oh why oh why am I so blue? Because when she looked into the lake in the still spring days, when she looked into its mirror surface all summer long, the only thing she remembers seeing is a ghostly reflection of her ghostly face, a ghostly reflection of a ghost of a face, a ghostly face she could never quite love, making an "o" with the "no" on the ghost on her lips, singing. There's no place like no place. There's no place

123°45'

at all,

as the clock on the mantle spins and spins, and she adjusts and orders and straightens herself reflexively, pulling herself jerkily tugging herself joltingly, not minding the fading, not minding the blanching, not minding the failing blue ink of time. She adjusts and orders and turns herself southeast by south to focus on the kettle, that black iron whistle of a kettle, to focus on the tea, that black iron tea with no milk and no sugar, to focus on the bread, that brown paper bread from the brown paper bag, that brown paper bread with no salt and no butter. She orders herself, pours the water, plates the bread, and turns toward the kitchen table stained by rings of condensation, that round kitchen table with its ring-shaped stains, that round kitchen table of rings, these circles within circles, spinning. Yes, she turns herself southeast by east, because this is the box in which she spirals. This is the box in which she beds.

She sits eating her bread and drinking her tea, but this is only a passing image. The more lasting image is that image from her long-lost past where her mother stands on the narrow path next that pebbly lake, that lullaby pond, that midnight, nightmare, heart attack pond, embedded with bone, and embedded with stone, embedded with the sharpest of shark-like teeth. Yes, the more lasting image is that image from her long-lost past where her mother stands riveted on that narrow, fixated and riveted and gripped as she watched her only daughter roll bits of bread with peanut butter, bits of bread with spreads of jam, bits of bread with marmalade into that pebbly midnight heart attack pond, once so still and motionless. Where her mother stands riveted on that narrow, watching the water as concentric circles begin to erupt, concentric circles begin to burst, concentric circles begin to spread and swell and multiply and divide, saying, No, saying, Nothing, saying, Nobody. Not even once. All on fire and full of flame.

She sits eating her bread and drinking her tea, but the more important image is the image where she crawls on all fours at the edge of that pond, barking like a dog, Come here, little fishy, Come now, my little friend, throwing bits of food to watch this still-life pond form rings and rings around and around this fleeting image of her long lost brother so full of love, this is the brother she doesn't remember ever having had, her long lost brother so full of lake, this is the brother she can't ever recall, remembering her mother once teaching her about something called surface tension in bodies of water. That in any drop of water, in any glass or thimbleful, in stony lakes or bony ponds, the water molecules on the surface of the body draw tightly and inward toward the center of the aggregation, toward the middle of the conglomeration, toward the heart of the matter, the belly of the body, the meat of the problem, forming a skin-like film resistant to upset. That the ripples that take shape on the surface of water, when the wind blows from whichever direction, *tramonta, levante, ostro, poniente,* are caused by this very force of tension.

And she wants to have been drawn inward toward the middle, inward toward the core, forever and always inward toward the center of the aggregation, toward the middle of aggravation. She wants to have stayed here and forever and always baying softly at the edge of the rippling pond, singing, Come here, little fishy. Come now, my little friend, but for her mother standing fixed on that path saying No, saying, Nothing, saying, Never, saying, No one. There's no place like no place. There's no place at all.

135°

For until development of the compass in the 11th and 12th centuries, position, destination, and direction at sea was determined primarily by the sighting of landmarks and by the observation of the celestial bodies. Ancient mariners often kept within sight of land for safety and for security. But the compass enabled the determination of heading into the obscurity of starless nights when the sky was hazed or fogged over.

One of the earliest references to a compass device, or a "magnetic direction finder," is recorded in the *Collection of the Most Important Military Techniques* written by the Chinese Wujing Zongyao during the Song Dynasty. In the *Collection*, Zongyao describes a "south pointing fish" floating in a bowl of water as he writes, "when troops encountered gloomy weather and dark and obscure nights, they make use of the mechanical 'south pointing fish.'"

During Zongyao's time, magnetization was likely achieved by the heating of common steel by a process known today as *thermoremanence*. Later, in the 12th century, mariners in both China and Europe made the apparently independent discoveries that lodestone is naturally magnetic and that, when floated on a stick in a bowl of water, aligns like the mechanical "south pointing fish" in the direction of the polestar. This discovery was quickly followed by a second discovery that a steel needle touched by a lodestone for a long enough period of time, it too aligns itself in a north-south direction. Eventually, the dry compass was invented and dispersed by piracy throughout the world.

In China, this dry version consisted of a wooden frame crafted in the shape of a turtle, and hung upside down by a board with a lodestone sealed with wax. The European version consisted of a freely pivoting magnetized needle fastened to a pin standing on the bottom of a bowl marked by directional points. At first, only north and south were painted on this bowl. Later, all of the thirty-two points were painted.

The Earth itself is a magnet with a north-south field that causes freely moving magnets to take on the same direction. The North and South Poles are ovals about 1,300 miles from geographic north and south. Lines of force connect the poles, and the compass needle aligns itself along these lines. Where magnetic north and true north coincide, the compass points to true north, although generally, the magnetic compass points a little east or west of north. The angle between true north and magnetic north is called variation, or declination. This wind rose, or compass card, is used to measure this variation on charts.

The wind rose is marked with directional pointers consisting of thirty-two evenly spaced points. The four cardinal points are north, east, south, and west, corresponding with the directions of the four winds, *tramontata, levante, ostro, poniente*. Between the cardinal points lie the primary intercardinal points of northeast, southeast, southwest, and northwest, *greco, sirocco, libeccio, maestro*. Secondary intercardinal points include north-northeast and south-southwest, and tertiary intercardinal points include north by east and south by west. The distance between each of the thirty-two points is eleven and a quarter degrees, and the naming of the thirty-two points in their clockwise order is called Boxing the Compass, *north, north by east, north-northeast, northeast by north*,

for those sailors cannot sail their ships who cannot with ease box their compass, *northeast, northeast by east, east-northeast, east by north*,

146°15'

east, east by south, east-southeast, southeast by east, twenty-nine one-thousand, thirty.

Because this is the center that never existed. Because this is the core that never was formed. Words still, not minding, her soliloquy, not noticing, her silhouette, here framed against the frame, framed at the box, at the table, framed against that spell, that shell, that hell of that moment, that dread of that dream, remembering and disremembering, *thirty-one one-thousand, thirty-two*, losing her rows of teeth.

Her rotation defines her orientation, as she sits at the edge of her broken table, as she sits at the edge of a broken piano, as she sits at the edge of a broken world, tossing bits of bread with peanut butter, bits of bread with spreads of jam. She was a child when it broke. Because

when she was a child she learned in school how to use her watch as a compass, her analog watch with the analog hour, her analog watch with the analog minute, that minute-by-minute version, conversion of this image illumined by the light of the flickering the lamp. She learned how to take her analog watch and hold it flat in the palm of her hand, and she learned how to point the hour hand toward the direction of the sun. She learned how to find the mid-point between the hour hand pointing toward sun and the twelve o'clock mark on her analog watch, and she learned that this midpoint between the hour hand pointing to the sun and the twelve o'clock mark, points north when she is in the southern hemisphere, south when she is the northern hemisphere, these circles within circles, circling.

And when she was a child, she took her analog watch with the analog hour to the analog path by the analog pond, singing, Come here little fishy. Come now, my little friend, to that mechanical south pointing fish. She held her watch in her analog palm toward the light of the sun, singing, Why am I so cerulean blue? Then she found the point between that long lost hour, that point between that long lost hour and the mark of twelve o'clock, these circles within circles circling. A wind rose. A wind rises still. Is rising now. For those children cannot sail their ships who can't with ease

box their compass. And though she would like the time to take a bath, instead

157°30'

she sits at the edge of her broken table throwing paper bread from a paper bag, throwing paper tea from a paper cup, throwing paper jam into the paper lake, all incendiary, and full of flame, until

up she tells her body. Up. Up, she tells her body, while the clock on the mantle spins and spins. For the only way out of this labyrinth is up. For the only way out of this maze is up. For the only way out of this puzzle, this flummox, this riddle, this quagmire, because the only way out of this jungle is up. So up she tells her body on her hardwood floor. Up she tells her body on her hardwood apartment. Up she tells her body in her hardwood world.

A wind rose, a wind rises, and she sends her body upward to face south-southeast, away from the table, its plate and its cup, away from this ocean, its kettle and stove, away from this lake so full of love. Because today, on this day, on this day of all days, she wants to write a letter to her mother, to her long-lost mother so full of life, a letter to her mother now rising like an angel, now flying like an airplane, now soaring like a dove in the cloudless sky. Because today, on this day, she wants to write a letter and send it to the sky in an airship, a rocket, a blue balloon. She wants to hire a skywriter, a highflier, a mercurial god. So up she sends her body across her hardwood floor, up she sends her body across her hardwood room, up she sends her body in her hardwood world, toward her wooden desk where she sits down at the edge of her wooden chair and draws a pencil from her wooden drawer to compose, to convey, and to tell.

Because the continental shelves are terraces of crust that abut the edges of landmasses and sink slowly seaward, then they stop sharply at their seaward edge with a steep drop called the shelf break. Below this break lies the continental slope, a deeper zone that merges with the abyssal plains

of ocean floor.

And the American oceanographer J.P. Swift called the shelves "palimpsests," tablets upon which things are written and erased, notebooks upon which stories are recorded and effaced. Each stand of sea composes a story of sediment, a story of silt, Not for the god. Not for the god, after the previous story has been eroded by the surf. For it's the surf that abrades it, it's the surf that reworks it, it's the surf that combs through everything as it passes, winnowing out the finer-than-sand-sized sediment, and leaving the coarser matter behind, like the shadow of a story, like the shadow of a shadowy god.

So up she sends her body across her hardwood world, not minding the clock, not minding its compass, and passing the mantle and the Macintosh Man. Up she sends her body, past the door, now opening and closing, to sit down at the edge of her erasable desk to write an erasable letter to her erasable mother, falling like a bird from the erasable sky, sinking like a ship in the erasable sea, lying deeper than deep in the erasable ground. Because she wants to write a letter to her mother, Dear Catastrophe, she wants to plant it, inter it, entomb it, submerge it. She wants to sink it, descend it, and bring it to naught. She wants to write an invisible letter, like the letter she got from her invisible brother, Dear Catastrophe. It's been a long time. I am writing you from the bottom of the deep blue sea.

For today is her mother's tenth anniversary. For today is her mother's hundredth anniversary. For today is her mother's thousandth anniversary, sailing like a song on the throaty sea, like a throaty oboe, like a broken piano, here, in her wooden world, where she folds herself up, limb by slow limb, and focuses on the pages. Words still. Mind clears. She starts

168°45'

writing, the word I, writing the word erase, with a thirsty spirit of fish and foam, winnowing out the finer than sand sediments, and leaving the coarser materials behind, inscribing and effacing, embedding and expelling, because this is the box in which she spirals, this is the box in which she crawls, this is the box in which she gnaws and paws across the page at the rate of the growth of a fingernail. Words still. Mind clears. She starts,

writing the word I, writing the word erase, for she wants to have been named by the lying down element, the selfsame element by which her mother was named, Dear Mother, I love you madly, I love you dearly, Mother Madly. She wants to have been named by the lying down element, but it's her name that keeps changing, this body of ocean and ocean floor. Words still. Mind clears. She starts

writing the word I, writing the word erase, remembering her dreams of ascents to heaven, remembering her dreams of her long lost brothers. Dear Mother. I love you madly. Mother Madly, I love you dearly, you who never bothered to dream some sleepy dream, because your life is dreamy enough.

Like a sailor who sails the lonely seascape, like a writer who wanders the lonely desert, she sits in her wooden world, with her wooden fists wrapped tightly around her wooden pencil, writing the words, I, et cetera, and erasing the words, I, et cetera, leaving only the shadow on the shadowy page, leaving only the echo on the words on the page, leaving only the shadow of the echo that carries the word. Like a writer she sits

writing the word I, writing the word erase, echoing the word I, echoing the word erase, and asking herself in all seriousness, asking in all earnestness, How far down this Nile do I intend to row? because she wants to contain her world into words, the ways and the days of her small unpleasant world, she wants to contain her world into words and send them madly to the grave. But instead, she sits with an "o" on the ghost on her lips, echoing, There's no place like no place. There's no place at all.

So she sits at the edge of her wooden chair and draws a wooden pencil from her wooden drawer, for here lies the bird, and here lies the box for the bird. Here lies the bird and, here, the box for the bird, for the only thing that makes a stone precious is its hardness, and the only thing that makes a star starry is its farness. She sits at the edge of her wooden world and starts, Mother Madly, It's been a long time. I am writing to you now from the deep blue bin so full of words, for no bird could ever love a tree properly, remembering and disremembering the petals of a flower, losing her rows of teeth, for no bird could ever love this deep blue bin, No, no one. Not ever, this deep blue bin

180°

so full of birds.

Words still, and her silhouette is framed in that spell of a world she could only dream of, losing her rows and rows. This gravity defines her orientation, as she sits staring at the edge of this wasted page, like she is sitting at the edge of the wasted sea, counting the letters of her wasted words, and thinking it's just a waste of time. For there is no moment more precarious, more unreliable, more unreasonable, than this image here as she sits still in her body of bone and of sinew, at her wooden desk of angle and line, writing and erasing, composing and effacing her words of wood, her words of stone.

Still words still, as if inside this living room there was only dying. Still words still, as if inside this living room there was only this slipping on this ribbon of time where birds keep falling from the sky, at thirty-two feet per second per second,

now flying, now soaring, now stalling and falling,

now turning her door-key counterclockwise in time, reversing the mantle, reversing her tea, turning her door-key counterclockwise in time, reversing the bread and the bits of jam, now marching backwards, now pressing toward, apace, apace, on this endless parade at her wooden desk in her wooden world, sitting and writing and erasing, effacing.

Still words still, not noticing the reflection in the window where the inverted image of her father stares back, not noticing the reflection in the window where her father now stands to the left of the man, the fawn-colored, rain-coated, Macintosh man. But who is this man in the Macintosh? Who is this brother of mine?

Still words still, then crossing it out, not noticing the inverted image in the window where the still-life bird is so precariously perched. There you are, mother. I love you madly,

not noticing in the reflection of the window where the ghostly clock reflected from the mantle spins its hands in reverse, turning away from this time, away from this place, in halves and quarters and eighths of a second, in this framed box window facing south, not noticing the space where she sits, between the clock on the mantle and the clock in the window, the space, the place where time and its reversal coexist and cancel each other out.

Because the more important point of view is the view from the moon where halfway around the world an airplane pilot, confusing his direction, turns an about face in the open sky. The more important point of view is the view where halfway around the world a commanding officer, doubting his capacity, calls about face under the drift of dawn. The more important point of view is the view where halfway across the ocean, a single sailor, tragic in his own catastrophe, turns an about face from the very helm that steers his boat.

So up, she sends her body, her stifling body of bone and of stone, moving toward some notion of movement, away from the desk, away from the page, and away from the window facing south. Because there is time for a bath today. Let there be time. Let there be space. There is time for a bath today, so she moves quickly, methodically, intently, precisely, out of the living room, through the hallway, into the bathroom, toward the clawfoot tub to take a clawfootbath. For on a rolling ship at night, by the light of the flickering lamp, the figure in the distance becomes visible as she

191°15'

fells her body the same way some people fell trees, for no bird could ever love a tree properly. She fells her body, branch by slow branch, limb by slow limb, listening to the somnolent memory of a wayward song. She was a child when it broke. She fells her old T-shirt that once belonged to her father, that poor heart attack of a man, that poor broken heart of a heart attack man, her father, her gilded father, who, if she remembers correctly, decided one day that he was going teach her how to swim.

I'm going to teach you how to swim, today, she remembers him saying, if she remembers correctly, by the swimming pool on some sunny day. Today, I'm going to teach you how to swim, in the backyard of a sunny ranch-style house. Mark my words, Silly Milly, you silly little girl. Today, you are going to learn you how to swim,

then he picked her up and tossed her swiftly into the still-life pool.

She fells her old T-shirt that once belonged to her brother, that mechanical south-pointing fish, that midpoint between the myriad hands of her myriad watch. I love you badly, brother bad, who, when she was a child, flashed, sparkled, and blinked from the bottom of the still-life lake.

She fells her old T-shirt, limb by slow limb, then fells her shoes and socks, socks and shoes, her belt and jeans, now bluing, now fading, as she gathers herself inside the shell of the tub, turning the handles counterclockwise, now hot, now cold, and

counterclockwise again, now hot, now cold,

and spills herself into that ocean predominating this world of ice and fog and lake and stream, smashing and thrashing in torrents of clouds, in tumults between phases, by evaporation, by precipitation, by movements of the atmosphere, and the downhill flow of memories that keep spilling through

this clawfoot tub in this clawfoot apartment, where ambiguous dogs bark as they bark and they bay as they prey to that invisibly rotating, orbiting moon.

And while she doesn't remember what happened next, she does remember the splash and the crash and the sinking down. She does remember the gasping, the panting, the frenzied breath. She remembers she couldn't scream. She remembers she couldn't cry. She couldn't open her mouth and crawl inside with, No daddy no. This pony can't swim.

Because there's a difference between taking it all and taking it all in. Like the difference between swimming in the shallows and sinking deep into the deep. Or the difference between surface currents and deep-water circulation. For when the wind blows over the sea, *tramontana*, *levante, ostro, poniente*, it causes currents to move in the upper layers of the ocean, *north, east, south, west*, but the surface currents don't move in the same direction as the wind, her mother explained, because of the movement from the spin of the Earth.

Don't you see, her mother said, surface currents move at an angle from wind, she remembers her saying, if she remembers correctly, in the backyard of some sunny ranch-style house. Currents in the upper ocean are caused by a combination of wind direction, *tramontana, levante, ostro, poniente*, and something called the Coriolis effect.

The Coriolis, that picture perfect palace, the Aurora Borealis, those arcs of light that ornament the poles. The Coriolis effect, her mother said shining like a lighthouse in the backyard of some ranch styled home, is the apparent arc of moving objects as seen from a rotating reference.

Imagine this, her mother continued, shining like a lighthouse, like a beacon, like a pharos, imagine two little children rotating on a merry-go-round in the park. Yes. Imagine you and your baby brother, for example, you and your baby brother, that silly little fish, imagine you and your baby brother standing on opposite sides of a merry-go-round going round. Yes. Now imagine that you throw a ball to your brother, that fishy little fish. Yes. You toss a ball to your pernicious little brother standing on the opposite side of a merry-go-round. Yes. If you toss a ball to your brother on a merry-go-round going clockwise, to you the path of the ball will seem to you to arc to sideways and to the left. Imagine that. But if you toss a ball across a merry-go-round going counterclockwise, the path of the ball will seem to arc to the right.

Now imagine that a strong wind comes from out of the blue, she said, now standing, rising, now higher and higher. The path of the ball will then be affected not only by the spin of the Earth, like a shining lighthouse in the middle of the yard. It will also be affected by the oncoming wind, like a beacon, a pharos, the Aurora Borealis. Currents on the surface of the sea work the same way, standing, then moving, then drifting away, moving in relation to the spin of the Earth and the direction of winds, shifting on the continental drift.

Whereas deep-water circulation, on the other hand, is caused by the upwelling and downwelling of waters.

Like the upwelling and downwelling of feelings. Like the upwelling and downwelling of emotions. Like the upwelling and downwelling of your deepest sorrows. Warm waters move down when they get carried to the colder climates, whereas cold water moves up to replace sinking, colder, denser waters, Wake up my little brother, for morning bells are ringing. Therein lies is a difference between taking it all, yes, taking it all,

and taking it all in.

And while she doesn't remember what happened next, after she tossed the ball toward her bouncing baby brother, while she doesn't remember what happened after the splash and the crash and the sinking down, she remembers she couldn't breathe. She remembers she couldn't see. She couldn't open her eyes and crawl inside with, No daddy no. This pony can't swim, while the rotating moon that orbits the rotating Earth, while this rotating moon

202°30'

turns blue.

Because here in the clawfoot tub of her arbitrary apartment she descends fully, overtly, pronouncedly, completely, reposing herself totally into the tomb of water, plunging her feet and her ankles and calves, her feet planting, her ankles bending, her calves flexing, her knees kneeling in the water, folding herself like an accordion, molding herself like a song,

sending her legs, her thighs, the center of her root, her belly, her middle, now softening, now yielding, relenting herself, her belly and trunk, settling her chest, her arms, elbows, and forearms, her wrists and her palms with their crisscrossing lines, her palms and her fingers, her fingers and arms, her chest and her breasts, her nipples now rippling in water, the color of wet terra cotta in the well-shaped shell, of unsung oak in the middle of spring, of a shiny penny in a wishing well.

She descends in the tomb of her shell, plunging her shoulders, her neck, her chin and her nose. She drops her head back to the porcelain edge, descending her earlobes and ears and the base of her skull. Then she looks at the ceiling painted the color of cloud white, hanging there for the briefest of moments, suspended, suspending, until she closes her eyes and holds her breath, plunging her head underwater, hook, line, and sinker.

She closes her eyes and holds her breath, plunging her chin and her cheeks, her mouth and her nose, her eyes and her forehead, and her the top of her crown, sending her tangle of hair floating in the tub like that floating seaweed that floats upon waves, like a web of webbing, like a mesh of meshing. She yields her body into the well of her clawfoot tub, closing her eyes and holding her breath,

yielding her body into the weight of the water, entirely, exponentially, mathematically, logarithmically, like she's plunging herself into the deepest sea, having walked the plank of her pirated past, having tossed herself in like a man overboard, she dives into that well, like she's diving into that spell, sinking deeper and further and farther and further,

thinking the word, I, thinking the word, erase, but for this flood that follows, thinking the word, I, thinking, erase, but for this flood that follows me home.

213°45'

Because blue light is shorter than red light, you see, so you see that everything near to the surface of the sea, everything near is blue. And while she doesn't remember what happened next, what happened after she was tossed, hook, line, and sinker into the new blue pool, she closes her eyes and holds her breath, reclining here in her clawfoot tub like she's reclining into the deepest sea, like she's reclining into the Atlantic, Pacific, like she's reclining into the Arctic, the Indian, the oceans combined, identified by their arbitrary margins behind arbitrary doors, now closing, now opening. She closes her eyes holding her breath, surrendering herself to the new blue din, to the sibilance of new blue sea, hearing the crash of one wave into another, to the thunderous hums of the rushing faucet, completely, profoundly, severely, and serenely,

deeper and deeper, steeper and steeper, eight, sixteen, thirty-two feet below the surface, sixty-four, one hundred and twelve, sinking into the sound

of the water rushing from the faucet, like she's sinking into the sounds of submarines and earthquakes and landslides, like she's sinking into the sounds of icebergs breaking off glaciers. She sinks three hundred, eight hundred, sixteen hundred feet deep, thirty-one, thirty-two, into the perfect zone, into the perfect channel, listening for the sounds of the sea emitted in halves, quarters, and eighths, *minim, crochet, quaver notes,* in eighths, sixteenths, and thirty-two seconds, *quaver, semi-quaver, demisemiquaver,* because this is the box of albatross and anemone, yes, this is the box of the humpbacked whale moan, this is the box of the dolphin love song, yes, this is the box in which she

spirals downward, spinning and twisting about, listening for the songs of her incalculable blackness, her indelible darkness, those songs of dolphins and snapping fish, as sound travels faster and farther in water than they do in air, her mother explained, because sound travels faster and farther underwater, increasing with depth, decreasing with temperature. Sound velocity in water is determined by the square root of elasticity divided by the water's density, and so she sinks completely in search of that perfect zone where sounds travel perfectly across the entire ocean, the perfect zone where sounds disperse horizontally across rather than in scattering directions, the so-called *sofar* zone, the zone in which whales and fish sing to each other, communicating and signaling location and direction, like birds that cry across the open sky, like beacons that flash across the open sea. She spirals downward searching for the so-called *sofar* zone thirty-two hundred feet deep, signaling

gently to her motherbrother, to her fathermother, signaling lowly her slow moans of lullaby and loss, with sounds of loyalty and sounds of reverence, like the sounds of a whale wailing, like the sounds of a sail sailing, like the sounds of the church organ she played as a child, with its thirty-two pedals and forty-seven stops, like the sound of the church organ she played on Sundays in her Sunday best, Not for the god but for those glorious songs, songs of hymn, songs of prayer, like the sound of the church organ she played with her mermaid wading in glowing peach. She closes her eyes and holds her breath to sing

gently to her motherbrother, tenderly to her fathermother, lowly and kindly, softly, adoringly, bravely across the plaintive sea, reaching with her small feet for one of thirty-two distant pedals, like she's reaching with her small fingers for one of one thousand distant stars, like she's reaching with her small ears for one fathomless, unspeaking god, singing lowly and slowly, sinking deeply, serenely into her well, into her shell, singing her unwed melody of the sunless sea,

while the rotating moon that orbits the rotating Earth, while this rotating moon

225°

turns blue.

Because blue light is shorter than red light, you see, so that one hundred feet below the surface of the sea, everything appears blue. The deeper you go, the greater the darkness. And while she doesn't remember what happened next, reclining here in her clawfoot tub, she sinks deep into the dark into the thunderous hum of that tenebrous black,

three hundred, eight hundred, sixteen hundred feet deep, past the twilight, past the azure, the cerulean blue and the midnight wine, past the *sofar* zone and further still, into the deep, into the dark, into the indelible blackness, the limitless, fathomless, into the consummate pitch, the dawnless gulf of the bottomless sea. She sinks deeper and deeper and steeper and more heavily into that yawning gape looking for the lights that stutter and stop, looking for the lights that flutter and flash. Like stars living stars in the dead of night. Like sands that shimmer on the desert floor. Like fireflies that flicker in the yards of those far away ranch-style homes, those ranch-style homes that spin around the spineless globe, those fireflies that blink and flick as daylight drops and nighttime expands, expanding. For at the bottom of the bottomless sea, her mother used to tell her, at the yawn of the dawnless sea, there is life that generates its own light. Yes,

life that generates its own light.

Like the flashlight and eyelight fish that beam and flare and flash. Like the cookiecutter sharks and anglerfish that glimmer and glint and glow. Like the viperfish. Like the pony fish. In their bodies, they release lights that flash, glimmer, and glow in the darkest deep. Like Morse Codes across the ocean floor. She falls falling to the dawnless sea, eyes closed and mouth yawning, like birds that fall falling, like rain that rains raining, like archangels who fall falling from heaven at thirty-two feet per second per second, like archangels who fall falling, looking for the light that matters, a gesture, a hint, a cue, slowly, looking for a signal, regretfully in search of her motherbrother, her fathermother,

for this is the box of phosphenes that flicker behind lids closed tight for sleep. Yes, this is the box of phosphenes that sink into the yawning gulf of the dawnless sea. This is the box of phosphenes that flicker and blink and wink in halves and quarters and eighths, yes, like the tick-tick-tick of the flint, like the drip-drip-drip in the sink. She closes her eyes and holds her breath because

this is the box of the those luminous sights that lull her off to sleep. Yes, this is the box of those luminous sights that lull her off

236°15′

to sleep.

and here she dreams about the end of time, and here she dreams about the endless sea, and here she dreams about the endless dress she wore as a child, the dress that would billow, inflate, and set sail, and those long lost sailors who wend their boats to sail toward the bent, impending edge of the ever offending horizon. She dreams of sailboats, and of steamships, and of clippers, and of sloops. She dreams of skippers and their captains, their dinghies and their rigs. And while she falls and fast to sleep, half a dozen fisherman lie buzzing in their bunks. Because these are the lights that lull her to dreams of explorers who set their sights upon the sea, buttoned up and zippered shut in summer whites and winter blues, like Sir John and Sir James in whites and blues aboard their majesty's majestic ships, like Sir John and Sir James aboard the Erebus and the Terrible, those ships named after the terrible and horrible, named after the dark and the abyssal, named after the endless sea that blows and flows to fills every nook on the expanding globe. She dreams Sir John and Sir James standing now at the helm of the Terrible tossing cannonballs over, tossing cannonball after cannonball to hear their simple wire soundings, cannonball after cannonball to map the bottom of sea, to map the bottom of this world. She falls asleep and here she dreams that she is dreaming, yes. She dreams that she is dreaming that she, herself, is bent at the edge of the Terrible staring severely into the shadowy sea, staring severely into that shadow of shape, cannonball after cannonball, Come here, my little fishy, come now, my little wish, like Sir John and Sir James tossing cannonball after cannonball clinging still to the abyssal floor, clinging still along with the skeletal bones of birds and fish, with the skeletal bones of whales and men, along the skeletal bones of those peppered sailors lost at sea on their lone bone ships that bellow in the dark, these lone bone ships of a pirated past, now sailing, now storming, now failing, now falling, at thirty-two feet per second per second, like dinosaurs dead at the entrance, like birds now buried in boxes, like the skeletal bones of mothers and brothers, and the skeletal bones of Atlantis,

the long-lost city of Atlantis, so buried at the bottom of the sea, that city of dreams, that city of nightmares, marvel of architectural performance and of concentric circles inside concentric circles, that marvel of engineering ingenuity, of concentric walls inside concentric channels, like the map of a Mandala or the map of a labyrinth. She dreams of being lost on a road. Like the map of a maze. Like the map of a daze. Because the only way out. Because the only way up. She dreams of swimming on a Venetian road. Like the map of a bird. Dead at the start. Like the map of the stars, an astronomer's chart. For though she admits it to no one, she believes Plato's retelling of the story of Atlantis to be a truthful account of a truthful city, a truthful city ruling in a muddy time, a truthful city ruling in a muddy world, until it sank truthfully into oblivion, the way she's sinking now, into the deep and into the dark, into the tenebrous black of the bottomless sea

punctuated by cannonballs.

She dreams of earthquakes and volcanoes. Of monsters and of dragons. Of seven heads and diadems and the sky rolling up like a scroll. For the plot of heaven, she knows from the Bible, Not for the god. Not for the god. The plot of heaven is perfectly cubed, these boxes within boxes boxing, with equal length and breath and height, twelve thousand furlongs long. But for the glory of the story. The plot of heaven is perfectly cubed, faceted with diamonds and paved with gold, gated by twelve glorious and perfect pearls.

Because this is the center that never existed. Because this is the core that never formed. She falls asleep, slowly, carefully, the way John fell asleep, and in her dreams she saw heaven and earth pass away, yes, the old heaven and earth pass away, and there was no more sea.

247°30'

She lies submerged in her clawfoot tub, immersed inside her clawfoot apartment, drowning in this clawfoot world, for this is the box in which she dreams of the humpback whale song, and of albatross and anemone, this is the box in which she dreams of assembling thirty-two petals and losing her thirty-two teeth,

until she wakes with a start in the new blue pool of some ranch-style house to the sound of a pistol, the sound of a shot, turning west-northwest on the arbitrary margin between sleep and wakefulness, defined more by history than by biology. She wakes with a start in the blue-green pond, that midnight nightmare lullaby pond, to the thunderous clap of the thunderous crack of that glaciated break under the weight of dreams. She wakes with a start in a pebbly lake with the pebbly crocs that chew rocks and hard stones to the sound of a woman whistling through a window, to the sound of a woman slamming the window shut.

She was a child when it ruptured, when it splintered and split, now she gnashes and flails and tosses about, now she splashes and lashes and writhes around, turning west northwest in her clawfoot tub, having sunk to the bottom of her clawfoot world, having crooned to her clawfoot mother and father, having crooned to her brother with evensong.

She gnashes and flails and tosses about in having submerged herself with the weight of dreams in a wishing well that sparkles and glints, with its blinks and its winks and its lullaby words, under ocean tides that recede and swell, under ocean tides that swell and recede, on this rotating Earth of desert and dearth. She was a child when it ruptured, when it splintered and tore. Now she wakes with a shatter and a slam in the tub to the bleat of loud birds and the barks of mad dogs that growl at the moon because

today is her mother's tenth anniversary, because today is her mother's hundredth anniversary, because today is her mother's thousandth anniversary, floating like a buoy at the edge of the tub, like a quivering quaver, a piano, here, in her clawfoot world, where she pushes her head expanding with water singing, Why oh why am I so blue? on the millionth anniversary of her mother's death,

bending her knees, planting her feet, flexing her calves, and gripping the edge, gripping the edge of the clawfoot tub with her two blue fists, her two blue fists with their white-knuckled grip, lifting her waterlogged chest higher and higher and her waterlogged spine further and further, sending her root and her thighs up out of the water, her root now rising, her knees, now kneeling, now flexing, now extending to ascend her skyward into her new blue world.

For today the millionth anniversary of her mother's death, flying like a dove out the broken window, here, in her new blue world, where she rises higher to step up out of the tub, stepping one foot, and then the other, onto the bathroom floor embedded with bone and embedded with stone, embedded with those beautiful hexagonal lattices, those beautiful hexagonal sea foam tiles,

on one foot and then both feet planted as she reaches for the towel hung on the hanging wall, like she's reaching for the box to bury the bird, to bury its body, to bury its flesh, to nurse it to health by the nursing way of those wire cannonball soundings. She dries her flesh with the sea foam towel and turns toward the sea foam corner to reach for sea foam clutter as she dons her jeans, one leg at a time, as she dons her shirt that belonged to her lover, as she pats the side of her mouth with her new blue towel and looks for a spell in the reflecting pond, as she looks for a spell in that reflecting glass, as she looks into the mirror of shadow and shape,

into that shallow glass of the most shallow shadows,

because she wants to have been a photographer once, shooting thirty-two hundred-speed film, she wants to have been a photographer once, shooting frame after frame after frame after frame, looking into the shallow mirror of more shallow shadows, like she's looking for her brother, her father, her mother, with her sailor blue eyes looking at herself like she's looking for the shadow of that which disappeared.

But then suddenly she remembers with a most sudden convulsion, like a cannonball shot from a seafaring cannon, the dream she had of losing her teeth, that dream of losing her canines, her molars, incisors, all with the suddenness of the most sudden blast, like the sudden awareness of a world gone bad, as she begins to count her teeth, like she's counting the petals off a red wind rose, like she's counting the moons from her fingernails, like she's counting the "o's" from the ghost of her lips, twisting her tongue turning west-southwest, west-southwest, gulping, convulsing, and gasping for air, Don't worry mother. I'm coming home.

258°45′

peering into the mirror, like she's searching for her mother, for her long lost mother at the bottom of the blank, searching for her mother, and reaching for her comb, then combing her hair in the clockwise direction, unknotting the knots, untangling the tangles,

combing and remembering that when she was a child, her mother combed her knotty hair with brisk rough pulls.

Ouch, my hair hurts.

So silly, Silly Milly. Why, your hair can't hurt. Why, your hair is dead,

looking in the mirror, combing her hair, and wishing for an internal compass by which to find her way home, like the internal compasses of moths that fly above her head in the middle of the day, like the internal compasses of monarch butterflies that flutter and start in the afternoon, like the internal compasses of bats that find their way darkling around the darkling globe.

These compasses help these creatures navigate their way in the absence of sun, in the absence of moon, that moon that orbits the orbiting Earth making the bulges and dips of high and low tide.

Sunless she peers. Moonless she seeks. Lifeless she searches the mirror longing for an internal magnetic compass, for those children cannot sail their ships who can't with ease

box their compass.

BOXING THE COMPASS

She looks *true north* into the mirror, with its zero degrees Kelvin, the perfect point at which ideal gasses have zero pressure, as they contract and cool, as they cool and contract, stopping all dynamic motion to achieve zero kinetic energy, and turns *north by east*, and its eleven degrees odd, because her mother used to comb her hair when she was a child, in the coral colored bathroom of the some bungalow, and when her mother used to comb her hair, she would say, Ouch, my hair hurts, and her mother would say,

So silly, Silly Milly. Why, your hair can't hurt. Why, your hair is dead,

and when her mother used to teach her how to swim, when her mother used to teach her how to swim instead of her father, she said the very same thing, I'm going to teach you how to swim, today, Silly Milly, but instead of tossing her hook, line, and sinker, she threw treasures into the deep end of the pool, sea glass, malachite, and zirconium, *north-northeast*, twenty-two degrees odd. She threw them in one after the other, and the treasures she found, scooped, and brought to the surface were treasures she would then save in her treasure box pirated from the pirated sea. She dove at these times to the deep end of that pool, *northeast by north*, and held her treasures in the shell of her hand, for that's what she called her, thirty-three degrees odd, her precious little fish. From the bottom of the pool, she looked up, eyes wide and blood red, she looked up to the blue sky refracted in blue sunlight, to the sunlight so scattered and skewed. She looked up through the warps of waves to the warping faces, and listened for the warping sounds of her singular name, Come here. Come now, my precious little fish. For the kettle on the stove is warming. For the waters of the world are rising. Come here, come now and forever, or until you disappear, *northeast*, forty-five.

But the first time she disappeared, she was in the foyer of this ranch-style house. She remembers this clearly. She was playing hide and go seek with her brother, her beggar baby brother, and it was her turn to hide and his turn to seek, so she hid in the foyer of the house inside a wooden box, a trunk, a wooden box with a metal latch, here inside her wooden world, *northeast by east*. She hid inside this box for minutes. She hid inside this box for hours. She hid inside this box for days. Until one day, her mother opened the box and found her fetal *east-northeast*. She opened the box and said with a quiver, Why, my little fish, do you give me such a fright? Why, Silly Milly, do you frighten me so? And she said, Don't worry, mother Madly, I'm getting along nicely in the dark. For here lies the bird, and here lies the box for the bird. Here lies the bird and, here, the box for the bird, for the only thing that makes a stone hard is its hardness, and the only thing that makes a star starry is its farness. Shadows, on the other hand, shadows are pleased, *east by north*, shadows are pleased, seventy-eight degrees odd,

with everything,

as she looks in the mirror for the shadow of her brother, she looks into the mirror for the shadow of her mother, as she strains her ears to hear their songs through the chirps of those birds now burning through the leaves, through the chirps of those birds now burning through the trees, through the chirps of those birds now burning through this ambivalent window where that ambivalent sun rises daily, *true east.*

And there's a photograph of her brother that was shot at thirty-two hundred–speed film. She remembers having seen it. She remembers it well. Framed within a frame. Boxed within a box. And when she was a child, she looked for her brother, so full of lake, behind the washing machine in the sunroom, thinking, Boxes are pleased with boxes. Only boxes are pleased with boxes. So she climbed over the washing machine and into the crawl space behind it because that's where she heard him, chirping like a bird in a broken piano, like the chirps of sweet birds, now flying, now falling. She crawled into the crawl space until she heard, Not now. No, no one. Not ever, Milly, never,

east by south, east-southeast, southeast by east,

she heard, No. She heard, Nothing. She heard, Never. She heard, No one. And she wanted to open her mouth wide and crawl inside. There's a picture of my brother the size of thimble. There's a hole in the sky the size of a symbol. There's a wind that blows, *southeast,* and a temperature that keeps on rising, one hundred thirty-five degrees even and rising higher.

Because the second time she ever disappeared was in the amusement park near the colonial house, *southeast by south.* Her mother had said,

We are going to amuse ourselves, today, Silly Milly. We're going to amuse ourselves in the amusement park. The day was sunny. The day was bright. She was standing next to her mother, and her mother was standing at a counter. She was standing next to her mother at the ice-cream stand. And while her mother was paying the ice-cream man, she wandered away, *south-southeast*, to the merry-go-round with tiny horses, to the merry-go-round cordoned off by rope, to the merry-go-round cordoned by the shape of a square. She wandered away, *south by east*, one hundred sixty-eight degrees odd, to the merry-go going, and mounted the tiniest merry-go horse, with a merry-go gallop and big green tail. She mounted the horse and closed her eyes to feel the bob and the sway of the round round world, to the feel the bob and sway of her winding world. And while she was galloping around and around, she felt like a pirate adrift on the water. And while she was galloping around and around, she felt like a lost mermaid in the open sea. And while she was galloping around and around, there exactly she was galloping around, with her eyes shut tight and her breath held taut, merry going and going, until she felt that familiar,

merry going, then gone,

true south.

And she remembers a dream that she had with her brother. And she remembers in the dream what her brother had said, *south by west.*

Now. You put a little in. You take a little out. You put a little in. You take a little out. So how are things changing?

minim, crochet, quaver notes, blank.

And she remembers another that she had as a child. A dream about climbing a crescendo of stairs, a *quaver, demiquaver, semi-demiquaver,* about climbing a crescendo of creaky wooden stairs in a house she never knew, *south-southwest,* two hundred two degrees odd. She was climbing stairs to the highest room, like she was climbing a wall, a wall of wind, higher and higher and louder and louder, like the trumpeting birds of the sweetest soprano. Higher and higher and louder and louder until she reached, at last, the highest door. Inside, she found the room was filled with boxes. She thought to herself, here in this room, there are too many boxes. There are too many different boxes, in too many different sizes. Then, she walked across to the corner of the room, the cluttered corner strewn with the smallest of boxes. She walked to the clutter and asked herself quietly, What small boxes are these? What small things do they hold? She sat and opened a box, the smallest box for the smallest of birds, and while she was sitting there, cross-legged and full of flame. When she opened the box, she didn't feel that she wasn't sitting in the four-storied house. She didn't feel like she was sitting anywhere at all. And by not being anywhere, she felt like she was home,

southwest by south, southwest, two hundred thirty-six degrees odd,

southwest by west, west-southwest,

and rising.

For when she was four, her father gave her an amber necklace that broke off from her neck. When she was eight, he gave her earrings that infected her earlobes. When she was sixteen, he gave her a hat, a tight felt hat that was right as day, until one day it was blown by the wind, *west by south.* And she chased that hat that was blown by the winds down city streets and across broad causeways, down broad avenues and across long bridges. She chased and chased all four winds in order to find her way home, *true west.*

I want to go home, *west by north.* I want to go home, *west-northwest.* She used to say that when she was a child, over and over, like a broken piano, like a broken Victrola, over and over, I want to go home, *northwest by west,* three hundred three degrees odd. Because she always had this feeling that she never quite made it. Like she was never quite home. Like there was some other place. Like there was some other place to be. And her mother would say, but you are home, Silly Milly. This is where you were born. This is where you live. She heard this over and over as she circled her world in the ranch-style house. As she navigated its territory and circumscribed its boundaries. As she tried to understand her home, her abode of snow.

Because the third time she disappeared was in a department store near the very same house, in halves, quarters, and eighths. She got lost amid the racks of clothing hanging pendulous from their wooden hangers, wandering around and around, until she hid under the hem of a whirling dervish of a skirt, that whirling dervish that billows, inflates and sets sail over the solo sea, *northwest.* She saw blue skies soaring ahead and blue waves undulating blue, with warm sunshine scurrying over zirconium horizons, sailing solo toward horizon's edge, merry going, merry going, three hundred fifteen and rising, merry gone, *northwest by north.*

She is the ambiguous daughter, in search of a brother. She is the ambiguous daughter, lost. And she told her father once what she wanted to be. It was night, and they were looking at the star-bright sky. She said to her father she wanted to be an astronaut in space. She said she wanted to fly with the twinkles of gods and their monuments. She said she wanted to soar. She said she wanted to sing. Like a skywriter, a highflier. And what he said was this,

Don't be rash, little thing. We are all lost on this boat. And the waters are rising, rising higher,

north-northwest, north by west, three hundred forty-eight degrees odd.

Because she wanted to be named by the falling down element. I'm Milly Fast. I'm falling fine. I fall quite nicely in the dark. Because that's the law of falling bodies. That they fall from the sky at a speed of thirty-two feet per second per second, which is slower than the speed of sound. They fall at a speed of thirty-two feet per second, squared, which is slower than the speed of sorrow. Thirty-two feet per second per second. It's the time falling bodies take to fight. Down to the ground. With gravity.

270°

And as she slams the door to her forgotten apartment, she walks west toward the occident. And as she slams the door to her forgotten apartment, she walks west toward the setting sun. And as she slams the door to her forgotten apartment, she walks west toward Hesperides, toward the islands of the damned. She slams it again and again in a spot in her mind, until she remembers suddenly, as the most sudden deduction, until she remembers suddenly, as the most sudden eruption, she remembers suddenly as the most sudden concussion, that she forgot her keys in her fading blue jeans, that she forgot her keys and their counterclockwise degrees, that she forgot her keys in her forgotten apartment in this quiet, reluctant, forgettable world facing west.

She slams the door to her forgotten apartment, having changed into her black and funeral pants, not fading, not blanching, not losing their hue. She slams the door to her forgotten apartment, having changed into her black and funeral shirt that once belonged to no one else. She slams the door. She slams the door again. Again and again. She starts walking, rhythmically, steadily, she starts walking methodically, the same way fishermen walk in their fishermen dreams, over the overlaps of planks, over clinker built hulls. So much like a sleepwalker. So much like a daydreamer. So much like a steady, unswerving ghost. Because today there is time. Because today there is space. Because today is the tenth anniversary of her mother's passing, floating on a raft in the far out sea, like a broken piano all out of true.

She slams the door to her forgotten apartment remembering with the remembrance of one who remembers the long lost letter that remains unwritten, remembering the shadow of the letter, written by the shadow of her hand, written on the shadow of the page sunk in the shadowless sea.

Dear Catastrophe. I'd like to take a long walk in a park. I'd like to find a straight path, unwinding, unbending. Because the only thing of which I am certain is the dignified insistence of the straight line. From point A to point B. From here until catastrophe. From now until calamity.

As she spirals in circles, in freeform infinities, down the ambiguous hallway where lines connect barks to echoes to shadows reciting and repeating the shadow of her letter,

Dear Catastrophe. I'd like to take a straight walk in a park. I'd like to walk along a straight and unwinding path until I come across the trunk of a large felled tree. And when I come across the trunk of a large felled tree, I will look at its rings and start to count. Then I will look to the sky and wonder if it was going to rain. And if it's already raining, I will look to the sky and wonder if it was going to clear up,

walking in spirals, in free-form infinities, past the mail collected in the broken blue bin, past the pile of papers stacked in the corner, past the cork board on the starboard bow, with the fading sense that she's forgotten something, that she's forgotten her keys in her fading blue jeans. She walks toward the closing door that opens wide, now closing, now opening, now buckling herself up, and locking herself out, now spilling herself onto the threshold of her ambivalent west-facing world,

where she stands

281°15'

nailed at the edge of her building the same way mermaids stand nailed on bows of ships, turning her ear to the dangerous waves that chop and swell in her box, in her bin, on this big blue street. She stands nailed at the very edge of her boxlike world the same way mermaids stand on the bows of boats, in this big, in the box, under the big blue sky, turning her eyes toward the silvery sea that slips toward the shimmering edge. She stands nailed at the edge of the edge of her box the same way crocodiles stand at the end of their ropes, baying and preying to her faraway god, beseeching and pleading to the invisible god, entreating and appealing to the incomprehensible god to grant her a safe voyage, a solo voyage now safe and sound,

a solo voyage underground.

And if there are any signs on the street that read, "Not For the God," and if there are any signals that blink, "Merry Going and Going," and if there are any symbols, figurations, a moral, a myth, she doesn't notice, standing like a mermaid at the helm of the boat. If there are any crocodiles snapping, if there are any whales beseeching, if there are any dinosaurs diving, if there are birds, any birds, if there are any good birds, lying in puddles of blood, lying in a puddle of blood dead at the entrance, if there are any good birds, now flying, now soaring, now stalling and falling, she doesn't notice at all,

Merry gone,

because the only thing she marks, the only thing she notes, she only thing she minds is the shadow of a ball rolling toward the street, the shadow of a ball toward the shadow of a street followed by the shadow of a child rushing behind the shadow of the ball, the shadow of a child rushing behind the shadow of a ball followed by the shadow of a dog barking on a leash, the shadow of a dog barking like a shadow followed by the shadow of a woman crying, Going, then gone.

And if there are any signs, any symbols, any beacons that flash, a red red ball rolling toward the street, if there are any omens, or forewarnings, or gestural crests, a child dressed in blue behind a rolling ball, if there are any codes, those long and short dashes of Morse, a dog on a leash barking in front of the shadow, the shadow of a woman so out of true,

a red red ball, rolling toward the street, and a child dressed in blue, rolling behind it, a dog on a leash flailing and scaling, and a woman disappearing, having missed her cue, until she descends from the edge of her edge, her edge, to walk west by north toward the underground rail,

thinking the word, I, thinking the word, fly, thinking the word, I, thinking the word, fall, if I ever am a steel bird. If I ever am a good box. If I ever am a red ball rolling in the street. If I ever am a ball rolling toward a far away world. I really ought to be more careful. For only boxes are pleased with boxes. Only boxes of boxes are pleased with boxes of boxes. Shadows on the other hand,

shadows are pleased with

292°30'

everything.

She walks west-northwest as the slow wind blows, imparting its weight to the increase of waves. As the wind gains strength, the waves gain strength, and the surface of the sea moves from ripple to flood, building in speed and duration and fetch. The points of the compass come from the direction of the wind, and the Chinese divide the rose by *rat, rabbit, horse*, and *rooster*. But the first thing to know is her name. Silly Milly. She's falling fine. Into the hollow of the underground rail. But the first thing to know is her nominal direction, so on a rolling ship at night, by the light of the flickering yellow lamp, the figure in the distance becomes visible as she

frames herself in the frame of this city where blocks become piled upon other blocks. She frames herself in the frame of the grid where buildings pile upon other buildings. She frames herself in the frame of this box where she feels most at home

in no place at all. The figure becomes visible framed in this tight void of a world where she plucks the petals off the compass rose, losing her rows of teeth. Her rotation defines her orientation as she turns west-northwest into the underground station, as she turns west-northwest through the underground turnstile, as she walks west-northwest through the underground sea of people, these people of parallax, these people of pull, to descend on the escalator to the underground rail.

You put a little in.

Because today is the trillionth anniversary of her mother, floating like a buoy at the edge of the escalator, floating on a raft in the dead dead sea, floating by the escalator she slowly descends, saying, Watch, Milly, now, as the slow wind blows, for when the slow wind blows, it forms waves upon the face of the deep, and, Isn't it funny, Silly Milly, floating on a raft, that before Beaufort, at the edge of her mind, before Beaufort standardized his Beaufort scale, one man's stiff could be another man's soft. Yes. One man's brake could be another man's swell. Because before Beaufort standardized his Beaufort scale, mariners measured the wind and waves by parallax and by pull.

You put a little in. You take a little out.

Until that funny little Beaufort, that indignant little Beaufort, that insistent little Beaufort with his mechanical little mind, until that the magnificent Beaufort had the magnificent wish to rid the world of ambiguity, to correct the world of subjective objectives. So that no man's soft would be another man's stiff. So that no man's story could be another man's song. So that no man's land could be another man's home. He wanted a standard, a system, a formula, coordinates, he wanted to organize and mechanize and set to scale

the ways of the wind and the ways of the world,

so that on a rolling ship, when the wind is calm, the surface of the sea is flat like glass, like the mirror I hold in my hand, see? Like the mirrored waters of Narcissus and Echo. But when the wind blows its low trombones, waves begin to rise, rise higher and higher with foamy crests that spread and spray. And when the wind blows its slow bassoons, the edges of waves drift and shift and sea foam blows in dainty streaks. And when the wind blows its tumbling trumpet, sea foam sprays up high and low, left and center, blowing with the winds that blow. And when the wind blows its hurricane song, sea foam covers, sea foam blankets, sea foam buries all you see on the fathomless ocean of thunder and sway. See, this is when your mariner, your single sailor lost at sea, this is when your only brother is blinded by the sight of white,

as she reaches the bottom of the escalator and pushes her body through the moving commuters, that sea of people, of parallax, and pull, as she reaches the bottom and pushes her body toward the pedestrian stage between two tracks, as she pushes her body to the stage and turns to watch for beacon lights from the fathomless dark, from the infinite, from the oncoming train, all the while remembering her mother telling her of the Beaufort's winds, all the while remembering her mother telling her of Beaufort's gales, while

one person looks at her,

and another one looks away.

303°45′

You put a little in.

You take a little out.

One person looks at her,

then another and another.

Her rotation defines her orientation as she sits at the edge of her orange seat at the very edge of a silver train, on her orange seat on a silver train moving in circles toward the cemetery, moving in circles toward the graveyard, moving in circles toward the long lost city of the sunken dead.

She sits at the edge of her orange seat the same way sailors sit at the edges of planks, not noticing the fleeting scene through the see-through window, not noticing the scene through the silver frame, that fleeting scene of disabling cables, those unsteady cables of wire and rust, twelve thousand furlongs long, remembering that it was Socrates who said, yes, it was Socrates who asserted that when a man is out of his depth, whether he has fallen into a pool or into the middle of a stormy ocean, when a man is out of his depth, he learns to swim all the same.

She sits at the edge of her orange seat the way sailors sit at the edges of planks not noticing the landscape of cables of wire but minding instead the moons on her nails, the waxing moons that wane as they wax, that waning moons that wax as they wane, because the shapes of her moons are still, because the shapes of her moons are steady. Because she's remembering her grandmother Luna and that silly digital gift. Because her nails still grow, are growing now, like the continents that drift and shift. She sits on the runaway train that starts and stops again, on the train that stops and starts and stops, while above ground in the boxy city, while above ground in her boxy world, while above the boxes of building and brick, a small white plane take flight.

315°

tuning, time and again she doesn't notice these things as she exits through the open doors of the train, now opening, now closing, now pushing her body through the parade of people, like she's pushing her body through a parade of paralysis, that dull population of parallax and pull.

One person looks,

but she doesn't see, because the only thing she sees, pushing her body, the only thing she notes, pushing and pulling, the only thing she minds, mounting the escalator, is that a slow wind blows now on the land.

Because, her mother told her, the scale was later adapted for use on land, with correct correlations between numbers and rotations, to avoid ambiguity, to avoid uncertainty,

so that on a rolling ship, when the wind is calm, smoke from a fire rises straight in a line toward that great big sky of cerulean blue. But when the wind blows its low trombones, smoke begins to shift and drift to mark the direction of the wind. And when the wind blows its slow bassoons, leaves of trees in suspension rustle in their world of green. Secret notes drift and float in winding scurries near the ground. And when the wind blows its tumbling trumpet, twigs and branches prance about. Light flags swell and sway and wave. And when the wind blows its airy flute, big trees sway. Smaller branches break and fall, piling on this boxed crescendo. And when the wind blows its hurricane song, cars begin to veer off roads, slipping, sliding on the streets, crashing, smashing one by one. And when the wind blows and blows and blows, signs on streets, those barricades and detour signs topple over, fly about. Roofs begin to curl from rooftops. Asphalt shingles break, begin to fly. Now they are flying, now they are soaring, falling, like birds that fall to the ground with gravity. See, this is when your winded pedestrian, this is when your winded brother, this is when your winded citizen tips his wings against the air, taking flight against the wind.

He takes his course upon the wind and starts

writing the word, I, writing the word, am, writing the words, coming, and, home.

326°15'

Outside she walks.

On the sidewalk she walks northwest by north.

Outside, on the sidewalk, she turns northwest by north in her city, concrete composite of heaven and hell, of sky and of sea, of mud and of boulder, of river and plane. Outside on the sidewalk she walks with cinderblock sighs under the looming skies of those crocodile times when she walked northwest by north with her mother, her brother, her shadowless father, that corpse of a puppet, that heart attack man, her mother, her brother, that crocodile boy crying crocodile tears at the edge of the pond, her brother, her mother, her mother Madly, with her distant eyes, for miles and miles in her sick world of body and block, of roundabout loop, of muscle and gape, like a clock, like a compass, like that mechanical fish, walking toward the edge of the page, baying and preying to an invisible god.

Outside, on the sidewalk, she walks in her sick city, in her uncivil city of illness and waste, where the waters are rising, are rising now, with the rising pollution that rises inside her, that pollution of lake and of lullaby pond, that pollution of dreams and their nightmare fish. And she wants to have been a bricklayer once, laying row after mechanical row, oh, but for the world, oh, but for its ways, oh, but for the wind that's blown it to bits.

And she wants to mark the scene of the crime with a marker, a tombstone, some tape, or a brick, oh, but for this calamitous ocean floor.

Good morning to you.

Good afternoon.

Outside she on the sidewalk she walks for miles and miles, twelve thousand furlongs long, through her blown up city of soot and of smog, where the wind is blowing its hurricane gust, where the wind is sewing its boxed-in storm, where the wind is throwing its knotted weight on everything in her sick city of scattered horses and merry-go-rounds.

She walks and walks in her city, blown to bits, shredded to threads by gale force winds, where cars now veer across the road, those silver, red, and burned up cars, spinning round on one way roads, where roofs are folding, caving in, those asphalt, shingle, paper roofs, that fold right up and unfold down, where one-way signs, those fleeting signs, those barricades and detour signs, topple up to spin in air, topple up to missile down, where windows burst dispersing glass, where trees uproot, and light poles fall, where chimneys fly and porches spin, where fences whirl and wind about.

Because this piles of bricks is not a house. Because a stack of sticks is not a chair. Because all the sand in the world couldn't make a castle. And she aggress with Aristotle that if the art of shipbuilding were in the wood, we would have ships by nature.

She wants to have been named by the lying down element. She's Milly Fast. She's falling fine. Because she wants to have been named by wings and tails and feathers and vents. Because she wants to have been named by the simpler song now flying, now soaring, now stalling, now falling. Because she wants to be named by the children she sees at the edge of her mind, those children she sees who bury their dead, those children who bury their dogs, with blown up barks from line to vine.

She's Milly Fast. She's falling fine. You put a little in. You take a little out. She's swirling around in her smashed up world, swirling on the sidewalk and crying out loud, for though she speaks to no one at all, Now, now, don't worry. I'm getting along nicely in the dark,

in this dark world of these dark times. In these dark times of blinding space.

337°30'

Because hurricanes, typhoons, and cyclones are different names used in different parts of the world for the same violent winds that move in a circles over the horrible and the terrible. They develop from the heating of the sun on the surface of the sea. This heating causes warm air to rise and create a spot of low pressure at the surface of the sea. And as the low pressure sucks in air, it sends it spiraling centrifugally to the center, creating a circular wind system that spins around and around like merry-go-rounds that spin around and around, counter-clockwise in the north, and clockwise in the south, due to the Coriolis effect.

But at the center of these hurricanes, typhoons, and cyclones is a calm area of low pressure called the eye. Around this eye, lies a space called the eye-wall where the air spins up and up. And it is in the eye, within the eye-wall, where single sailor, lost at sea, can be found folding, can be found unfolding, folding and unfolding, folding and unfolding, in nautical circles by the nautical clock.

And it is in the eye, within the eye-wall, where Silly Milly, lost at sea, can be found looping the compass, that cold wind rose, in simple "o's" and figure eights, those free-form infinities in the cemetery by the lone stone sea, looping the compass in the cemetery, that lone stone maze of grave and of wave in some sinking plot for the sunken dead. She loops it once, she loops it twice, she loops the compass again and again all amid those stones of morning and of woe,

looping the compass in free-form figure eights with her weeping tones of thrust and throttle, in search of the shape, in search of the shadow, in search of the memory that makes her stay.

348°45'

Because she wants this way forever to stay, because she wants this way forever to sway. Because she wants this way forever to say, This is where I am standing. This is where I am slanting. On this line that connects and does not intersect. On this ridge. On this bridge. On this sky-line bridge over the ocean bay.

This is where I am slanting. This is where I am pitching. This is where I am tipping. This is where I am winging. And she wants this way forever to stay, yes, she wants this way forever to say.

If I ever am a steel bird. If I ever am a brown box. At thirty-two feet at thirty-two feet per second per second. If I ever am a red ball toward the distant horizon, at the edge of this bridge, thirty-two feet per second squared. This is where I was born. This is where I live. But for this flood that follows me home.

ACKNOWLEDGMENTS

Gracious thanks to Brian Kiteley, Robert Savino Oventile, and Vincent Standley for their committed support of my work. Thanks as well to Letras Latinas for making this book possible. Thanks to Caldera Arts, La Muse, and Headlands Center for the Arts for providing the space and time. And finally, thanks to my good parents, Mario and Millie Florian, for their eternal and unfailing encouragement.

ABOUT THE AUTHOR

A Latina writer, Sandy Florian is the author of **[speak
& spell]**, *On Wonderland & Waste*, *Prelude to Air From Water*,
The Tree of No, *32 Pedals & 47 Stops*, and *Telescope*.